Barbara Bottner and Gerald Kruglik

Illustrated by Olof Landström

KATHERINE TEGEN BOOKS
An Imprint of HarperCollins*Publishers*

Wallace's Lists

www.harperchildrens.com

Library of Congress Cataloging-in-Publication data
Bottner, Barbara.
Wallace's lists / by Barbara Bottner and Gerald Kruglik ; illustrated by Olof Landström.— 1st ed.
p. cm.
Summary: Devoted to making lists about everything in his life, Wallace the mouse discovers the joys of spontaneity and adventure when he becomes friends with his neighbor Albert.
ISBN 0-06-000224-7 — ISBN 0-06-000225-5 (lib. bdg.)
[1. Mice—Fiction. 2. Friendship—Fiction. 3. Spontaneity (Personality trait)—Fiction. 4. Orderliness—Fiction.]
I. Kruglik, Gerald. II. Landström, Olof, ill. III. Title.
PZ7.B6586Wal 2004
[E]—dc21
2003008431

Typography by Jeanne L. Hogle
3 4 5 6 7 8 9 10
❖
First Edition

For my father

—B.B.

For Valerie and Geoffrey Kruglik

—G.K.

Wallace, a mouse, could do almost anything. Anything, that is, as long as he had a list.

He kept a list of all the clothes in his closet. That way he could get dressed in the dark and everything would match.

Wallace had lists of pets he would like, stories he loved, and exciting weather, such as thunderstorms, hailstorms, and blizzards.

When Wallace woke up, he wrote a "to do" list. This morning it read:

Wallace watered his plants.

Then he rang for the elevator.

"Hello. My name is Albert," announced Wallace's new neighbor.

Wallace would have liked to say, "Hello. My name is Wallace," but saying hello was not on his list.

Wallace wondered what Albert was like.

The next "to do" list Wallace wrote read:

So Wallace introduced himself to his neighbor.
"Would you like to listen to some music?" asked Albert.
"I have to do my laundry," Wallace explained.
"Laundry is laundry," said Albert, "but music is life!"

Wallace thought of Albert as he watched his clothes tumble around in the washing machine.

When Albert called out, "I'm off to paint some ducks," Wallace wished painting was on his list.

Later that afternoon, Wallace saw Albert's painting in the hallway. Something had gone wrong.

Wallace knocked on his door. "Where are the ducks?"

“I changed my mind,” Albert boasted.
Wallace was dumbfounded.
“Changing my mind is an adventure,” Albert explained.
“I don’t like adventures,” said Wallace.
“An adventure can be anything. Anything that isn’t planned for.”
“You mean anything that isn’t on a list?” asked Wallace.
“Exactly!” said Albert.
“Do you ever use a map?” Wallace continued. “I have lots of maps!”
“I don’t need maps,” said Albert, “because wherever I go, there I am.”

"But what if you get lost?"
"Being lost is *automatically* an adventure!" cried Albert.
"Suppose you get lost and then fall down and hurt yourself?"
"I pick myself up and keep going," replied Albert.
"When I get in an accident, it makes me feel better to write a list," said Wallace.

Wallace showed Albert list #3.

#3

Accidents that happened to me:

1. Bumped my nose while vacuuming.
2. Scraped my knee (same day as bumped my nose).
3. Stubbed my toe.

"Excellent," said Albert. "Perhaps you would like to join me sometime?"

"If I ever *did* go somewhere," said Wallace, "it would be to a place from list #7."

#7 Places with funny names:

1. Katmandu.
2. Mali: Timbuktoo.
3. Walla Walla.
4. Glockamorra.

"Glockamorra! How 'bout tomorra?" cried Albert.

"To be fair," explained Wallace, "there is one more list you should know about."

#8 Things I hate:

1. Rain streaming down my glasses.
2. Sand in my shoe.
3. Being hot.
4. Being cold.
5. Being wet.

"And especially . . ."

6. Being lost.

"Hmmm. It *is* quite possible that at least one of those things might happen if you went to Glockamorra," Albert admitted.

Wallace agreed to think about it anyway.

That night, the idea of an adventure made Wallace so nervous he couldn't sleep. When he finally dozed off, it was dawn.

Wallace awoke to the sound of rain plinking on his window.

He thought that on such a dreary day he might like to share some nice onion soup with Albert. He looked at his recipe.

Wallace only had two onions. Perhaps Albert had one to spare.

On his friend's door he saw a note:

Wallace watched the sky grow darker and heard the rumbling get louder. A major storm was heading their way!

Torrents of water fell from the sky. Wallace had to warn Albert about the dangerous storm.

Wallace had to make his way to the airport before his friend took off. He unfolded his map and waited for the bus.

Before he knew it, he was drenched. His glasses streamed with water. His map was soggy.

If this was an adventure, he sincerely hoped he'd never have one again.

At the airport, the Arrivals and Departures board was the biggest list Wallace had ever seen. And it was changing right in front of his eyes. He would have enjoyed just standing there and watching it flicker, but first he had to find Albert.

He raced from terminal to terminal.

He got caught on a baggage belt and tumbled around with the suitcases.

In Terminal 3 he was chased by a cat.
Wallace rushed outside and a bus splashed water on him.

Wallace decided to go back inside and climb up to the observation deck, where he could see almost everything.

No planes were taking off or landing, so perhaps his friend was safe.

Then he noticed a sad-looking fellow.

Albert!

Wallace was thrilled that his friend was safe. He told Albert how his map got soggy, how he didn't have his rain goggles, and how he was bumped around on the luggage belt and chased by a cat.

"Wallace, you had a real adventure!" Albert exclaimed, but he didn't say much more, since his own adventure on the *Rapid Rodent* had been cancelled.

Wallace remembered a list he read in the newspaper:

But Albert was not heartened by these remedies.

Wallace had one more idea. He took Albert to the baggage claim. They held onto each other and rode around the conveyor belt until they were dizzy.

They hopped onto a fancy piece of luggage that was loaded onto a trolley and led outside, where it was then heaved into a huge limousine.

They watched the city lights whiz by.

When the limousine stopped at a giant building on Park Avenue, Wallace whispered, "Let's go inside!"

Wallace and Albert rode up the elevator to the thirtieth floor, stepped onto the balcony, and gazed down on the whole city.

"We are almost as high as my plane," said Albert. "I can see just as far. And it's not bumpy. Thank you, Wallace."

"I wish I had a steaming bowl of onion soup," said Albert when they arrived home.

Wallace was just about to tell Albert he needed three onions to make proper soup when he decided instead to just chop up the two onions he had and put them in water. Then he sprinkled in some sugar, even though it wasn't in the recipe.

As the soup simmered, Albert found Wallace's list #11.

"How about Cincinnati?" Albert suggested.
"My Aunt Hattie lives in Cincinnati," said Wallace.
"Do you really have an Aunt Hattie?"
"Of course not!" laughed Wallace.
Telling jokes had never been on any of Wallace's lists.

Onion soup with only two onions was delicious.

When Albert went home, Wallace made a new list.

My adventures: #13

1. Going to the airport in the rain.
2. Getting lost.
3. Being chased by a cat.
4. Rolling around on the conveyor belt.
5. Riding in a limousine.
6. Being on Park Avenue balcony.
7. Making onion soup with only two onions.
8. Telling a joke.

It was a long list, the longest list Wallace had ever written. But it was not nearly as good as list #14.

My best friend:

1. Albert.

That was his favorite list ever.